GET READY...GET SET...READ!

WHERE IS THE TREASURE?

by
Foster & Erickson

Illustrations by
Kerri Gifford

BARRON'S

"Oh no!" says Jan.
"Look at this club."

"What?" asks the dog.
"Not now," says the hog.

"I know what we can do.
Lets make the club look
brand-new," says Jan.

"Not me," says Kip.
"How?" asks Pip.

"I have a plan," says Jan.
"I'll be back as fast as I can."

"What is Jan's plan?"
asks the dog.
"Here she comes," says T.J. Frog.

"Here," says Jan.
And she hands her plan to Stan.

"Let me see," says Stan.
"Jan's Treasure Hunt."

"The hunt can be as much fun
as the treasure," says Jan.

"Let's go, let's go!" says Pip.
"But where do we go?" asks Kip.

Hint 1: Where some like to **jog**
Look for a log in the . . .

"**Bog!**" calls the hog.
And away they all jog.

But when they get to the bog
they cannot see the log.

So they all lend a hand
and make the bog
the best in the land.

Hint 2: Where the small **band** found a tan can in the . . .

"**Sand!**" calls Pip.
And away they all skip.

But when they get there
they cannot see the can.

So they all lend a hand
and make the sand
the best in the land.

Hint 3: Look for the tub
and make it look **good**.
You will find it in the . . .

"**Woods!**" calls Kip.
And away they all zip.

But when they get to
the woods, they cannot
see the tub.

So they all lend a hand
and make the woods
the best in the land.

Hint 4: **Rub-a-dub-dub**
now you must **scrub**,
to find the treasure in the. . .

"**Club!**" they all call.
And away they all go
to the club.

"We will never find the
treasure with the club
like this," says Kip.

So they all lend a hand
and make the club
the best in the land.

"Do you know what, Jan?
The hunt was fun," says Stan.

"But Jan, where is the treasure?" asks T.J. Frog.

"Look around!
Think of all the treasures
you have found."

Dear Parents and Educators:

Welcome to **Get Ready...Get Set...Read!**

We've created these books to introduce children to the magic of reading.

Each story in the series is built around one or two word families. For example, *Frog Knows Best* uses the OG word family. Letters and letter blends are added to OG to form words such as JOG, BOG, and SLOG.

This **Bring-It-All-Together** book serves as a reading review. When your children have finished *The Tan Can, The Best Pets Yet, Pip and Kip, Frog Knows Best,* and *Bub and Chub*, it is time to have them read this book. *Where Is the Treasure?* uses the characters and words introduced in Set 2 of the **Get Ready...Get Set...Read!** Series (Each set in the series will be followed by two review books.)

Bring-It-All-Together books provide:
- much needed vocabulary repetition for developing fluency.
- longer stories for increasing reading attention spans.
- new stories with familiar characters for motivating young readers.

We have created these **Bring-It-All-Together** books to help develop confidence and competence in your young reader. We wish you much success in your reading adventures.

Kelli C. Foster, Ph.D.
Educational Psychologist

Gina Clegg Erickson, MA
Reading Specialist

© Copyright 1995 by Kelli C. Foster, Gina C. Erickson, and Kerri Gifford

All inquiries should be addressed to:
Barron's Educational Series, Inc.
250 Wireless Boulevard
Hauppauge, NY 11788

ISBN-13: 978-0-8120-1098-5
ISBN-10: 0-8120-1098-1
Library of Congress Catalog Card No. 94-38559

Library of Congress Cataloging-in-Publication Data
Foster, Kelli C.
  Where is the treasure? / by Foster & Erickson : illustrations by
Kerri Gifford.
    p.   cm. — (Get ready—get set—read!)
  Summary: While they are hunting for treasure, the animals in a
club clean up the bog, the sand, the woods, and their clubhouse.
  ISBN 0-8120-1098-1
  (1. Animals—Fiction. 2. Cleanliness—Fiction. 3. Litter
(Trash)—Fiction. 4. Stories in rhyme.) I. Erickson, Gina Clegg.
Clegg. Get ready—get set—read!
PZ8.3.F813Wg   1995
(E)—dc20   94-38559

PRINTED IN CHINA
19 18 17 16 15 14 13 12 11

There are five sets of books in the

Series. Each set consists of five **FIRST BOOKS**
and two **BRING-IT-ALL-TOGETHER BOOKS**.

SET 1

is the first set your children should read.
The word families are selected from the short vowel sounds:
at, **ed**, **ish** and **im**, **op**, **ug**.

SET 2

provides more practice
with short vowel sounds:
an and **and**, **et**, **ip**, **og**, **ub**.

SET 3

focuses on
long vowel sounds:
ake, **eep**, **ide** and **ine**, **oke** and **ose**, **ue** and **ute**.

SET 4

introduces the idea that the word family sounds
can be spelled two different ways:
ale/ail, **een/ean**, **ight/ite**, **ote/oat**, **oon/une**.

SET 5

acquaints children with word families that
do not follow the rules for long and short vowel sounds:
all, **ound**, **y**, **ow**, **ew**.